THE MAN WITH A LOVELY DOG CALLED PEBBLES

The Life of an Assistance Dog for the Disabled

Written by Pebbles

(Assisted by Jack Porter)

Copyright © 2016 Jack Porter
This book is sold subject to the condition that it shall not, by way of trade or otherwise, be lent, resold, hired out, or otherwise circulated without the publisher's prior consent in any form of binding or cover other than that in which it is published and without a similar condition including this condition being imposed on the subsequent publisher.
The moral right of Jack Porter has been asserted.
ISBN-13: 978-1530278626
ISBN-10: 1530278627

DEDICATION

This book is dedicated to Andy and Jenny Clarke of Woofability without whom dogs like Pebbles and all his friends would not be helping so many disabled people today.

CONTENTS

Chapter 1 .... *1*
Chapter 2 .... *4*
Chapter 3 .... *7*
Chapter 4 .... *11*
Chapter 5 .... *15*
Chapter 6 .... *19*
Chapter 7 .... *22*
Chapter 8 .... *26*
Chapter 9 .... *29*
Chapter 10 .... *35*
Chapter 11 .... *40*
Chapter 12 .... *43*

ACKNOWLEDGMENTS

Thank you to Martha Cooke for the wonderful illustrations of Pebbles at work.

Chapter 1

I am a Golden Retriever and I am an assistance dog for people who are disabled in some way and need some help every day. My name is Pebbles; I am called that because when I was a puppy I was sponsored by a school in Gosport. When you sponsor a puppy you get to give them a name. To sponsor a puppy is a really generous and wonderful thing to do because to get me and all my friends through our training costs a lot of money. Anyway, the children at the school in Gosport had a shingle beach behind their school, hence the name Pebbles. When I was growing up the people at WOOFABILITY started to train me in lots of things that normal dogs do not get to do in their lives, and this is why we are all looked on as being special dogs doing special things to help disabled people. After my training was completed I was three years old and could do lots of things, so was then ready to be placed with somebody who needed me to help them. This is where it gets very important that I remember everything I have been taught so I can make a difference to somebody's life. One day I was put in the car; this was not new to me because as part of my training I live with people who are known as socialisers. I had different ones in my early life because that made it easier for me to get to know lots of different people, which has made it easier for me as life has gone on.

Anyway, back to my story. Andy took me in the car this one day, it seemed like we were going for ages (Andy drives slowly!!), but eventually we arrived at our destination which

THE MAN WITH THE LOVELY DOG CALLED PEBBLES

was Colehill and we went to a door and rang the bell. The door was opened by a man who I now know to be Roger and he was the man I had come to help, and did he look like he needed it!!! They let me look around his home which was very nice really and I thought to myself, *You have landed on your feet here, Pebs mate.* I know I am lying down!!!!!

Chapter 2

I woke up next morning to look around my new home; in the hall was the front door and I saw that Roger had a newspaper delivered. This was my chance to impress him, so remembering my training, I went to the door and using my mouth, pulled the newspaper through the letterbox. We Retrievers have very soft velvety mouths so I did not damage the newspaper and I took it through to the bedroom where Roger had awoken and presented him with his paper. He was thrilled that I had done this for him and gave me a biscuit and a pat, thanking me for being so clever. I had done this for him because in the morning it is very difficult for Roger to move about due to his Parkinson's disease. How wonderful it is for him and other people who cannot get around very well that Woofability train us dogs to help them do these things that everybody takes for granted.

Not long after I had got Roger his paper I heard the key in the door. *Who is breaking in?* I thought. So I went to the door to investigate and to protect my new responsibility, and there was a young lady called Linda. I heard her shout to Roger that she had arrived. Linda was Roger's carer and she and her colleagues came every morning to get him washed and dressed which was one less job for me, I thought. When Roger was washed and dressed she sat him down and fed and watered him, after which she came over to me and made a fuss of me. She was very nice and I was very happy that I was with Roger because everybody was so friendly, and I had had two hugs and a biscuit and it was not even nine o'clock yet. It turned out that Roger had three carers a day to help him get lunch and tea, so I would meet two more of his carers later, but that's another story I will save for later.

Chapter 3

One day Roger was not very well and he had to go to the doctor in Wimborne. After Pip, his carer, had got him up and washed and dressed it was my turn. NO!!! She did not wash me, I do a very good job for myself thank you very much, but he does have to dress me. I have to wear a special red body jacket because if I have not got it on Roger is not allowed to take me into any businesses in town that he has to visit, anyway it makes me feel special when I, Pebbles the assistance dog, see other dogs and they have not got a jacket like me. On my jacket it says I am from Woofability and I am giving independence to the disabled, this tells shopkeepers and shoppers that Roger and people like him need me and my friends to give them a better life. After Roger got me ready he took me on my lead to his car and I got in the back on my special blanket so we could go to see his doctor. This was the first time I had been in his car and it was very nice and comfortable, I must say.

When we arrived at the doctor's and had parked the car, Roger opened my door and I jumped out to be with him. This was all new to me, I had never been here before so had to be very observant, so if I came here again I could help Roger as I would have been before. Roger's Parkinson's makes him very unsteady on his feet, so I have to make sure he is safe and does not fall over. We walked through the car park to some doors which were automatically opening and closing, and led Roger through them safely. The doctor's waiting room was at the end of the corridor and after Roger had checked in I led him to a small sofa so he could sit down. All of the time I could feel lots and lots of eyes staring at me. People were talking to Roger about me and stroking and patting me, we assistance dogs get used to all that you know, and it is nice for the people we assist to have the attention because then they do not feel awkward or left out.

A door opened in the corner and a man who I now know to be Roger's doctor called him through. This was exciting, for I had never been to a doctor's surgery before and it certainly was very busy; the doctor was very nice and Roger told him who I was and why he had got me. The doctor was pleased that Roger was getting some help, which is what he needed badly. After Roger had finished we went back home and I lay on my blanket thinking about the exciting day I had with Roger at the doctor's surgery.

Chapter 4

After all the excitement of yesterday I awoke on my blanket wondering what was going to happen today. I had not got long to wait to find out how it was going to begin, because the door opened and in came Linda. You may remember I told you that because Roger has Parkinson's he has a carer to help him get up in the morning, well one less job for me, so no complaints from Pebbles!! Linda is very nice and always makes a fuss of me (can't blame her, can you?). Sometimes if Roger is really poorly she evens feeds and waters me, now that's what I really call CARING!!!!

After Roger had finished getting ready he took me for my morning walk. This is the best bit for me because I really get to stretch my legs and get some fresh air. Where Roger lives there is a nice small wood across the road and he takes me in the wood for me to do what we dogs do first thing, but he always puts it in a bag and takes it home so other people do not tread in it, which is very nasty and gives us dogs a bad name. We then walked home as it had started to rain and I HATE GETTING WET!! Roger has to towel me dry and then it takes me ages to preen myself all handsome again. The only good thing is I get to lie in front of the fire which is magic!! I lay there thinking what Roger will get me doing later. I did not have to wait long to find out.

I heard him call my name and I got up, stretched after the warm fire, and trotted off to find him. On went my red Woofability jacket and my red lead so I knew straight away I had some work to do, because if you remember I told you if my red jacket was on I was going in a public area where Roger needed my help. The best bit of this though, was that I got to ride on the back seat of the car. Woweee, how I like riding in the car. When I was safely in the car, off we went. *Where are we going?* I was wondering. It didn't take me long to find out as we drove into a car park and I saw the sign: 'Dentist'. Roger was going to see his dentist. *Good luck mate,* I thought. If it was anything like my dentist at the Vets he was welcome to it!!!!!!!!!!

Roger got me out of the car and we entered the big building where the dentist worked. We went in the lift to go up to the reception and Roger was told to sit and wait to be called. Just like at the doctor's lots of people were staring at me, then asked if they could stroke me as I was such a beautiful dog and so well behaved. That's my training paying off again and Roger takes care of me as well, so I am happy and content, just like it should be. It was not long before Roger was called to go in to see the dentist, I of course went with him and I saw a very big chair – the biggest I had ever seen ever – and there was the dentist and a very nice young lady who helped him. Roger told me to lie down in the corner so not to be in the way. I did as I was told then covered my ears with my front paws so I did not hear Roger screaming the place down!!!!!!!!!!! Poor old Roger, he was like a little boy because he hated the dentists so much, however after the dentist had found the problem Roger was finished and we left to go home again.

Well that was exciting, I have visited the doctor and the dentist in two days, now back to my blanket to think what excitement awaits me tomorrow.

I have told you lots of times about Roger's car and my favourite blanket that I lie on at home.

Here they are for you all to see. Looking at my picture, it is obvious Lassie is very much second when it comes to looks!!!!!!

Chapter 5

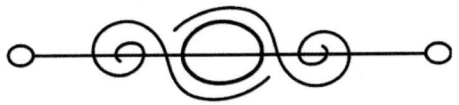

After I had my usual morning walk and Roger was ready, I had my breakfast. It could not have come any sooner; because of all my excitement of the day before I was STARVING!!! I was eating my breakfast very quickly as usual, this was a trick I had learnt as a puppy so I got more than the others, naughty but clever eh! Anyway, back to my story. I could hear this noise, like stones being thrown at the window. When I looked I could see it was raining very heavily. I could hear Roger moaning because as it turned out we were going shopping at the supermarket and it meant probably getting soaking wet. I had never been shopping before, not to the big shop anyway. I used to go with Roger to the village shop but never to the big shop, sounds like I am in for another exciting time. Never a dull time when Roger's about, that's for sure. I wonder if I will see any girl doggies. I hope he brushes me before we go, want to look my best, I will be fighting them off.

The reason I had not been to the big shop is because of Roger's disabilities – sometimes he is not well enough to go so he has to do it on his computer, they call that online shopping, very helpful to lots of people like Roger. I hope when we get there he does not leave me in the car with the window down so I have ventilation, it's lonely but most of all there is no excitement. I need not worry, he is getting my bright red jacket to put it on me, which means it's all systems go, I am going in with him. You may remember from before I told you that if my jacket is on I can go into shops and other places that Roger has to visit. It has stopped raining now so Roger gets his two shopping baskets out and puts on my lead and we head off for the car that is in the picture above. Oh I do like riding in his car, it is so comfortable, but I have told you all that before haven't I? Sorry to bore you, think I have caught it off Roger, listening to him going on to everybody about his car. His car, should be our car!!!!

It takes us a little while to get to the car park. Roger stops and says hello to some people who share the flats where we live, and when Roger stops and says hello, does he say HELLO!!!! Better to be friendly than the other way. He opens the back door for me and I jump in and lie down on my nice red blanket, then it's off we go. The road is very busy and it takes us over thirty minutes to arrive at the supermarket, and when I see this massive shop for the first time it takes my breath away and my long pink tongue hangs out of my mouth. WOWEE!!!! It's massive and the car park is very big as well. Roger finds a disabled parking spot and parks the car, he then gets his shopping baskets out of the boot. I am still waiting on the back seat, hoping he is taking me in. WHOOPEE! He is! OH how exciting, my first visit inside a supermarket. Roger gets his trolley from the long line of gleaming machines that are waiting for the eager shoppers and away we go. As usual Roger has a list with all the things he needs written on it. Hope he has some dog food, I don't want to go hungry, do I? Up and down the wide, long aisles we go, when suddenly Roger drops his list on the floor. Pebbles to the rescue! Without him asking, I very carefully pick it up for him, taking care not to rip or tear it. The floor is very shiny and is tiled, so it was difficult to get my mouth round it, but we Retrievers have very soft mouths and after a little while, mission accomplished and a grateful Roger gives me a pat and I get a little biscuit for being a good boy.

By this time a small crowd of people have gathered in awe, or in the aisle at least. Yes, I can be quite funny sometimes!! They ask Roger if that is normal and what else I do for him; they are all very interested and I have to pick Roger's stick up when he drops it to show them something else I can do. We eventually finish our shopping and at the checkout the lady cashier asks Roger all about me, so he tells her all about me. I think he is quite proud really, little does he know I like him a lot too. After paying the bill we leave the store and go back to the car. One thing I have noticed today are wheels!!!!!! They are everywhere and some of the trolley ones don't know which way they are going and you have to keep dodging them. Well it has been another very interesting day again but with all the excitement and the dodging of all those trollies I hope Roger uses the computer next time!!!!!!!!!!! What's going to happen tomorrow, Pebs mate? One thing, it can't be any worse, can it?

Chapter 6

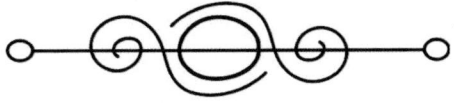

During the evening when Roger normally goes to bed and I am lying on my blanket, I could not help feeling like something was happening that fills a dog's brain with curiosity. Roger was not in bed, but in the store cupboard trying to get something out of its hiding place. When he had finished, there on the sofa was a large blue leather suitcase and next to that was my green holdall. *What, Pebbles, is going on?* I said to myself. *Don't say he is leaving me alone, but no, he cannot be because my bag is there also. And he would be lost without me to help him anyway.* Roger started to pack the suitcase with clothes and all his medication, and then in my bag he put my towel and mat, my two bowls to eat and drink from, special dog biscuits, and lead. He then turned out the light and went to bed. *What on earth is going on?* says I, a very worried doggie. I did not get much sleep that night, even counting cats never helped and it always did before.

Next morning, Roger took me out for my morning walk,

and Linda came to wash and dress him as always, but this time I heard a word I was not really familiar with. Linda said to Roger, "What time are you setting off on your holiday?"

Holiday!!!! What's a holiday? I was saying to myself.

"About ten o'clock, Linda," replied Roger. "It should only take me a couple of hours."

She asked him where we were going.

"Hayling Island, it's near Portsmouth," said Roger.

It dawned on me then why the two bags were on the sofa with our things in and I thought, *Brilliant, we are going away for the first time together. Oh what fun.* The bags were loaded into the car, and Roger put my lead and special jacket on, and opened the back door for me to lie on the back seat, but I was so excited not much lying down was going to be done. I wanted to see where we were going. It came to ten o'clock and Roger started the car and we began our journey to Hayling Island and our holiday was about to start. Wowee!!!! The journey was exciting; we went through places that I had never seen before. Part of the New Forest passed us by and then for the first time ever I was on a motorway. Oh goodness me, how fast everything was going!! There were cars, lorries, and all sorts of things I had not seen before. It was too much for a dog to take in so I decided to have a lie down on the back seat and enjoy the moment.

We arrived at Hayling Island quite quickly really, but I could hear Roger getting a bit angry so decided to have a peep through the window at what had annoyed him. There was a long line of traffic waiting to go into a caravan park on our right, but Roger needed to go into a holiday village where we were staying and the traffic was blocking the entrance. Patience is a virtue that Roger has not got a lot of, I am afraid. We arrived eventually at our holiday destination and parked the car near the reception area. Because Roger is disabled he has a special card which allows him to park the car in special areas so he does not have to walk far. From the very first moment we got out of the car I knew it was the place to be. "Oh what a beautiful dog, what does he do for you? How old is he?" and various other compliments were thrown in my direction. *Oh Pebs mate, hark at all that. For the next four days I think you are going to have the time of your life. Make the most of it,* I think.

Chapter 7

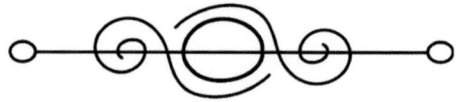

Roger reached the reception desk eventually after all the adulation for yours truly, and we checked in. They then showed us around the holiday village and we were shown to our chalet, which was to be home for the next four days as I have previously told you. When Roger had unpacked and got to know where everything was I was taken for a walk so I could make myself comfortable after the journey. On the walk I could see the boats all tied up in the harbour and we walked for a time on the coastal path between Hampshire and Sussex. I was thinking more on the lines of, *I hope he lets me off the lead, that water looks inviting!!!!* After my walk, or should I say our walk, Roger made way to get some refreshments for himself. When we sat down for him to have his drink and sandwich, lots more people came across and asked if they could stroke me and asked him lots of questions about me and what I did for him. He, as usual, sang out my praises and said that he could not be on holiday without me there, so I felt really special then. I always knew he was grateful for me but it is always nice to be told.

The next four days passed so quickly and did we have fun; during the day we would go off in the car to explore and we would find places to walk and for me to run around, enjoying myself. And then at night whilst Roger was eating his dinner I would be lying on the carpet behind him, dreaming of the day we had had and wondering what tomorrow would bring. After dinner there would be dancing and entertainment and halfway through Roger would take me out for my last walk of the day, which was ever so nice because walking down by the boats, seeing the lights twinkling in the water and the beautiful fresh air, set me up for the next day a treat. All good things come to an end and sure enough the holiday did, but before we loaded the car and set off for home Roger had one more place to visit, and it was a very important visit indeed.

There is a school on Hayling Island and they have been raising money for the charity, to be able to buy other dogs for people with disabilities like Roger. We found the school, which was not far from where we were staying, and arranged with the lady in charge to visit the next day. This we did, thinking that a few children would come to see me and stroke me and then we would go home. But when we walked through the doors, imagine our surprise to find there was a special assembly of the whole school to welcome us. Roger explained what disabilities he had and why he had an assistance dog to all the children and their teachers who had gathered in the hall. He then showed them what I did, showing them how I picked up the things he dropped and then how I fetched things he needed. And looking at them all, I must say they were quite impressed that dogs that they raised money for to help people like Roger were such a great success. After Roger answered questions and we had photographs taken with them all, and with the invite to come back one day and have lunch with them, we said our goodbyes and headed off for home. What a special way to end what had been a simply fantastic holiday.

Chapter 8

Three days after returning from our fantastic holiday, Roger had to go to the local hospital in Poole, this was to see a lady called a Parkinson's Nurse. She specialises in seeing people like Roger to talk over any problems they may be having. This was the first time that Roger had been to see her, and as I had never been to a hospital before I was quite excited. Usually Roger would have driven us to the hospital, but he was not feeling very well that morning so sensibly decided to ask for a lift from the hospital transport people, who were more than happy to help him because it would be too dangerous for him and others to drive that day. He may like a joke and a laugh most of the time, but he can be sensible when he wants to be, just a pity for me it is not more often. I mean I hear his jokes all the time and I think people laugh out of sympathy really. I am sure you would do if you had heard them, believe me. Just recently the cheeky devil has been saying I told him it, if they groan about a joke he tells.

Anyway, on with the hospital visit, I am beginning to sound a bit like him now!!

The car arrived to take us to hospital. I say a car but it was a large people carrier so that I could get in as well. I obviously had my special red jacket on that I have to wear when I am working, otherwise I would not be allowed inside the hospital with Roger. It took forty-five minutes to get there because the driver had to collect somebody else along the way, and when we got there, well, I was amazed at how big it was. Wowee!! There were lots of people dashing everywhere. We got to the department Roger needed to go to and when he had checked in at reception, sat in the waiting area to be called. As usual it was not long before I noticed people looking at me, smiling and nodding. Roger told the people who asked all about me and what I did, but then you all know that from what I have told you before, don't you? I of course just lie back and enjoy all the adulation, don't tell me you wouldn't either, because you did when you were smaller, you just did not realise it then.

Eventually Roger had his name called out and we went to see the special nurse who could help him. We were in there for quite some time but that was because the lady needed to ask Roger lots of questions because it was his first visit. And she got me a bowl of water as well, which I did enjoy. The man came to pick Roger and yours truly up as arranged and off we went home. Roger took me for a long walk when we got home which I did enjoy, because it had been a long day and I had been lying down most of it and wanted to stretch my legs. I was very impressed with my day at the hospital I must admit, I do not think I have seen so many people in one place before, and so helpful and friendly, just what the doctor ordered really I suppose. Yes, and that is one of Pebbles' own jokes, not one of his!!!!! What a way to end the day.

Chapter 9

Sometime later, Robin, who is Roger's brother, came round to the flat to visit. We do not see him very often, or his fiancée Jill, because they live quite a long way from us. I really love it when I see them because they are great company and spoil me with treats and long walks. Roger, with his mobility, cannot walk me very far, so it is a real bonus for me when Robin and Jill come because I know I am in for a treat. It is like my birthday and Christmas rolled into one. Anyway, on this occasion it was just Robin and he only stopped for a little while, and then after a short chat they shook hands like brothers do and off he went. What I did not know was a trip had been organised, that turned out to be possibly the best trip I had ever had.

It all started about three weeks later if I remember correctly, and us assistance dogs have to remember so much that sometimes we can get confused, not a lot, but a little. So bear with me, alright. Roger started one night to pack my green bag like when we went on holiday. *Oh*, says I. *Pebs, we are on the move again. Where to this time?* I thought. Roger also packed his suitcase, so I knew that wherever it was we were going, it was for a while. Roger loaded the car and then fetched me, and as you know I love going in the car, so no complaints from me; I jumped straight onto the back seat on my blanket and away we went. I looked out of the window and recognised the way we were going, it's the same road as when he takes me to the old airfield (which I will tell you about later on). It is also the same road that we take when visiting Robin and Jill, looks like I am in for a treat. Whoopee!!

We arrived at their house and Roger parked the car in their drive; the front door opened and Robin came out and they moved our cases into their car. *What's going on?* says I to myself, between the pats I am getting off Robin. I did not have to wait long for an answer though, out came Jill with some bags to put into their car, and then got into the back of the car with yours truly. *This is exciting,* says I, probably giving the game away with wagging my tail that much. Roger got into the front of the car and Robin into the driver's seat and *whoosh*, we were on our way. I was curled up on the back seat next to Jill. *Time for a little sleep*, I thought, so that is what I did. And I was fast asleep, eating this wonderful juicy bone, when I felt myself being shaken and Jill saying, "Come on Pebbles, wake up, time to get out now." We had stopped at a restaurant for them to eat some lunch, but as Roger needed me to help him to get to the restaurant and back my jacket was put on and then we could all go in together.

The restaurant was very nice and bright inside and we soon found a table to sit at so as to order their food. After they had finished eating it was time to leave so we all made our way back to the car and some more sleep for me, I hoped. I, of course, was in dreamland pretty quickly once we had started off again, with the movement of the car acting like a rocking chair. I still had no idea where we were going to but I love surprises, so was happily looking forward to it. When I opened my eyes after what must have been a long time because I felt really rested, I could see through the car window we were on a motorway like when we went on holiday.

We left the motorway not long after and Robin left the road and drove into the very large car park of a hotel. I could see from the sign that we were in Dudley, West Midlands. My memory is very good, which is why I am an assistance dog, and I remembered the last time I was in the West Midlands we all went to a football match in Wolverhampton. Robin, Jill, and Roger are fans of Wolverhampton Wanderers and we have come to see them play tomorrow and stay at the hotel for the weekend. Pebbles, as it turned out, was quite right, because when we checked in at reception I heard Robin telling the man that we were here for the football tomorrow. I had a lovely day when we came last time so started to get excited about tomorrow. *I hope they have brought my Wolves scarf that I wear. I love walking around with it on.* Our room was really nice, and Roger had brought my basket for me to sleep in, so it was just like being at home. But suddenly there was a problem. Roger had left his Parkinson's tablets at home!!!!!!!!!!!!!!!! He needed to get to a doctor to get some more but he did not know any, this was Dudley after all.

Robin of course, after that long drive, was none too pleased and who could blame him? *I am an assistance dog but packing is Roger's job so not my fault mate,* is what I was saying under my breath!! But to the rescue came Jill; she knew what to do, as she is a sister at a hospital. She spoke to a doctor on the telephone and arranged for us to pick up a prescription for the tablets and go to the chemist across the road from the doctor for the tablets. I stopped with Robin in the car when we got there, much warmer, and it's cold in the Midlands you know. Even for an assistance dog with lots of hair!!!

They were not long and when they got back Jill had got the name of a restaurant for tomorrow night from the man in the chemist. After dinner we were all very tired so went to bed, everybody looking forward to what should be an exciting day tomorrow. Tomorrow arrived and Roger got out of bed and took me for my morning walk. There was a big park at the back of the hotel so we went there and I had a good run around to wake up. After Roger had his shower we met Robin and Jill and all went for breakfast; the dining room was very busy because the hotel was full and while they had their food they discussed the day in front of us. Roger got the directions to the restaurant Jill had found out about, and Robin said we could find it before going on to the football. When we found it Roger went in and reserved a table and asked if I could go as well. "Yes," they said, "as long as he wears his jacket and he behaves himself." They did not know me. I am Pebbles, I always behave myself!!!!! We then went to Wolverhampton to watch the football, but the weather was so beautiful that before the game we spent a lovely time in the park sitting in the sun, then we went into a café.

Chapter 10

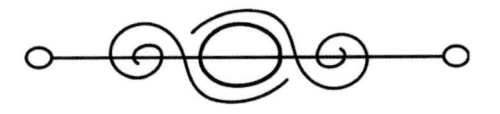

We walked to the football ground, which was only a little way from the park. But before we did we went back to the car, and they put their Wolves scarves on and then Jill put mine on. It is shorter than theirs of course, it goes around my collar and makes me feel so proud. I am sure my paws don't touch the ground when I have my scarf on and everybody looks at me smiling because I am the only dog in the ground with his own scarf and I am a Wolves fan just like them. Robin had told the club that Roger was coming with his assistance dog and they had organised places for us to sit in the disabled persons' enclosure. We walked around the ground before the game and people were saying hello and asking about me, and one man took some photographs of me. He was a special photographer and asked Jill about me. Whilst walking around I could smell this lovely aroma coming from a van. *That smells nice,* says I to myself. The man starting shouting, "HOT DOGS!!! Get your tasty HOT DOGS!!!"

That was enough warning for me to get out of there as quickly as I could!!!! Poor Roger had no alternative but to follow as quickly as me. He obviously had not heard the man in the van shouting.

Robin found out which gate we had to go through but they opened a large gate for Roger and me to go through, and we met Robin and Jill inside. We were then shown to our seats by a nice man who came down some stairs because they were waiting for us all. We could not have had a better welcome from Wolves if we had been royalty. We had seats right at the front so we could see the players easily and the two mascots of Wolverhampton Wanderers, Wolfie and his girlfriend Wendy, came and said hello, but until I realised who they were I was a bit taken aback by them. When the game ended it was a draw but the other team, Brighton, were top of the league so Wolves did well really. The important thing was we all enjoyed ourselves and we still had going out to the restaurant to look forward to. Oh what a great weekend so far. Now I have to get Roger back through all these people to the car, so excuse me for a moment whilst I concentrate.

Well we have all made it back to the car, but it was hard work for yours truly I can tell you. It is at times like this that an assistance dog comes into his own, because the pavements were full of people and crossing the road with all that traffic is a complete nightmare. But when people see me in my red jacket leading Roger they normally are very polite and move out of the way, or stop their vehicles and let me take him across the road safely. The journey back to the hotel was a short one, but took a long time due to the slow-moving traffic going home from the football, and people who had been to the shops. When we arrived at the hotel Roger, Robin, and Jill got ready to go out to the restaurant they had reserved that morning. We had a taxi from the hotel so they could have a drink and not have to worry about driving, which I thought was very sensible of them.

The taxi took us right to the door of the restaurant. Oh I was so pleased because it meant I had not got far to lead Roger – I still had not recovered from the walk back to the car from the football. The restaurant was an old cinema so I had to get Roger down the steps without him falling; there were six flights of steps down to the dining area so as you can imagine I had to be very careful indeed. A man in a very nice suit greeted us and showed us to our table. Roger said, "How did you know who we were? You never asked."

The man grinned and said, "We don't get many special dogs wearing special jackets come in here, so it just had to be you, who else!"

I went to my place under the table whilst they sat down. It

is important that I don't get in the way of the people serving so I always lie under the table. The restaurant was huge and served three different types of food: Indian, Chinese, and Italian, and it seated 700 people!!! Roger, Robin, and Jill all had Indian and you had to go and help yourself from big metal containers. Jill took Roger by the arm and helped him get his food four times!!!!! It was an 'eat as much as you want' restaurant, and Roger ate as much as he could, believe me. People were there having their birthday parties. I think they played 'Happy Birthday' at least six different times and everybody joined in singing it even though they did not know them!!!! I was having as much fun as they all were; this was new to me and I was enjoying it under the table resting.

We got back to the hotel quite late and everybody went to bed and I went on my blanket, curled up and thought, *What a fantastic day. I have been very busy doing my work but wow, have I enjoyed it all. Time to get some sleep.*

Next morning, Roger gave me my early morning walk and after they had breakfast, loaded the car. *Oh,* I thought. *We are going back home now.* How wrong could I be? They found some old tunnels that men had taken the limestone out of many years ago. You went into a boat, with a lot of other people, and went down the flooded tunnels to see where the men had been working all those years ago. It was very interesting but very cold so I was glad of all my hair to keep me warm, and I looked after Roger getting onto the boat and getting off in the way I had been trained to. It was not as easy as it sounds because the boat was bobbing up and down in the water as we got on and off, but nothing is too difficult for Pebbles so we had no problems or accidents. After we returned to the car, this time we were going home and what had been the most fantastic weekend for us all had come to a close. I lay on the back seat next to Jill (my favourite spot), eyes closed, thinking how good and clever I had been getting Roger up and down all those steps and crossing the busy roads without one bad incident. Cor, I am a clever dog you know, modest as well.

Chapter 11

You may remember me mentioning about an airfield earlier, and I promised to tell you more about it. Well I think that time is now. The airfield is about thirty minutes' drive from home and is an old Royal Air Force station now converted into farmland, with some three old hangers still standing. Apart from the exercise space for me, Roger likes to go because he was in the Royal Air Force when he was much younger, and I think it brings back some memories for him of what it was like. Of course he has the permission from the farmer to take me, and always takes away any mess I may make up there; don't forget I have told you before that it is very important to take it home. I have heard Roger many times talking to others that walk on the airfield and it was used to send the gliders across on D-Day, and when the attack on Arnhem was made in the Second World War. I love it there because he takes my lead off and I run and run and run on part of the old roadway. Quite often there will be birds pecking on the grass but when old Pebbles gets close to them they peck no more!! And do their impression of an aircraft taking off and flying away. Such fun! Whoopee!!!! I wouldn't hurt one really, just my idea of a bit of fun, honest. Because Roger has difficulty with walking he sits on a bench put there in memory of an old serviceman, and watches me enjoying myself, then when he thinks I have had enough he puts me back on my lead and we go back to the car.

I lie across the back seat getting my breath back whilst we make our way home again. I am very lucky to be with Roger because although I work very hard for him he really is the most unselfish man and lets me play hard as well as work hard.

Here I am proudly wearing my Wolves scarf.

Chapter 12

The next day arrived and after Marion, his carer, had got Roger out of bed and washed him, I was wondering what the day had in store for me. Marion left shortly after, and I heard the letterbox rattle – the newspaper had arrived. I dashed to the door and pulled the paper out, and took it in my mouth to Roger, who was sitting in the lounge waiting. After the usual "Good boy," and pat, he went to the cupboard and got me a well-earned biscuit. However, my busy day was just beginning, so it seemed, because instead of sitting down to read the paper, Roger went and got his laundry basket from the bedroom. *Here we go*, I thought. *No rest for the wicked or Pebbles today, it is washday!!* Let me explain to you what I mean. Where Roger lives there is a laundrette with washing machines and dryers, and this is where everybody does their laundry. Stands to reason I suppose, that is why it is called a laundrette!!!!

Anyway, as you know Roger has mobility problems and an

arm tremor because of his Parkinson's, so this is where I earn my corn, or in my case doggie food!!! He has a four-wheeled walker which he calls his chariot, and he places the basket on the top and we walk down to the laundry room. When he finds an empty machine he opens the door and puts the basket on the floor. This is where I come in, because to stop falling over, Roger sits in the chair on his walker, then I with my mouth pass him the washing piece by piece for him to put into the machine. After he puts his powder and conditioner in the tray comes the bit I like best – using my two front paws I shut the door ready for Roger to start the machine. We then go away and return to the machine when it has finished. This particular day we went back to the flat. I lay on my blanket as usual while Roger used the phone to call somebody, always on the phone, he is, but it is a major help to him. Because he is disabled and cannot get out and about as well as other able-bodied people, he needs to use the phone to organise his life. This call sounded interesting, he was making a reservation at his favourite bistro in the next town away, and I like going there because I get made a fuss of. Roger then read his paper.

After a while I could hear a noise further up the corridor from Roger's flat. *I recognise that noise,* I thought. *Like a metal banging noise. Got it,* says I. It was the postman coming down the corridor doing his deliveries. I got up from my blanket and strolled over to the front door.

"Where are you going Pebbly?" asked Roger. He could not hear the noise because he is deaf, poor boy. I got to the door just as the postman pushed the envelopes through the letterbox but could not catch them, so had to pick them up off the floor. I then took them to Roger who took them from me, amazed that I had heard the postman coming. I got a special pat and a nice biscuit for my brilliant performance. It was not much later that Roger called to me to go back to the laundry room as his washing would be ready to put in the dryer. Sure enough, on our arrival the machine was finished; now the fun begins. Roger opened the door of the dryer which was on a shelf above the washing machine, then opened the washing machine door. It was my job to take all the washing out and pass it piece by piece to Roger, and he would put it in the dryer. That sounds like hard work for a dog, doesn't it? Well it is, I can tell you, but I got three biscuits for doing it so mission accomplished. After about one hour, with the drying of Roger's washing complete and all nicely folded in his airing cupboard, he got ready to go out. *Oh yes,* thought I, *we are going to the bistro for lunch.* I had forgotten, due to all the hard work I had been doing that morning. I am not complaining, you understand, it is what I am trained to do, and I get restless and bored when there is nothing to do!!!

Roger finished dressing and then got me dressed in the usual fashion; you must know what I mean by now. Yes, that's right, red jacket first then my collar and lead, and then it is down to the car park for a ride in my favourite car. It does not take long to get to the bistro, in fact my blanket barely gets warm, and Roger has to use a car park around the corner. After he parked the car he opened the back door for me to get out, and then locked the car to keep it safe from burglars. It is only a ten-minute walk to the bistro from the car park but I have to concentrate because we have to cross the road twice, and the pavement is rather narrow. We arrived safely and entered the bistro to a lovely welcome. "Hello, how are you? You are looking so well and very smart as usual." They then said hello to Roger!!!! Then showed him to his usual table in the corner. It was out of the way, and I had plenty of room to lie down which is the main thing. Because he was driving, Roger ordered a soft drink and they brought him the menu.

It was at this point that the main door opened, and a well-dressed lady entered the bistro; she closed the door behind her and turned facing the tables. She looked in our direction and spotting Roger, she exclaimed in a loud voice, "I know you, you're the man with the lovely dog called Pebbles!"

At last, I thought. *Fame. Now I do know how Lassie felt!!!!*

Printed in Great Britain
by Amazon